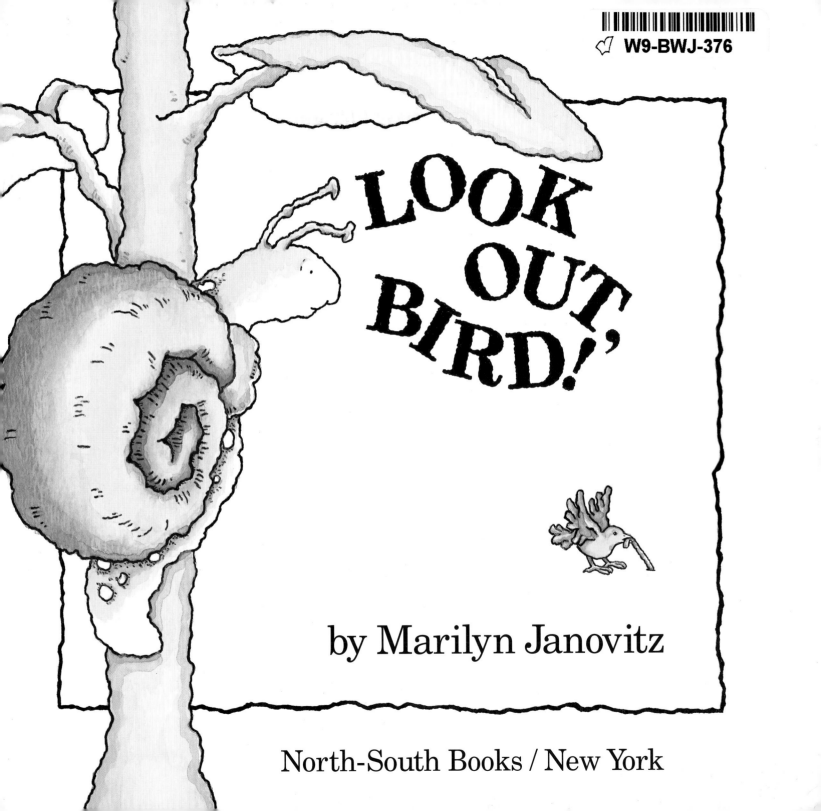

LOOK OUT, BIRD!'

by Marilyn Janovitz

North-South Books / New York

Published in the United States by North-South Books Inc., New York.
Published simultaneously in Great Britain, Canada, Australia, and New Zealand
in 1994 by North-South Books, an imprint of Nord-Süd Verlag AG, Gossau Zürich,
Switzerland. First paperback edition published in 1997.

Library of Congress Cataloging-in-Publication Data
Janovitz, Marilyn.
Look out, bird! / by Marilyn Janovitz.
Summary: A snail starts a chain reaction involving many animals
when it slips off a branch and hits a bird.
[1.Snails—Fiction. 2. Animals—Fiction.] I. Title.
PZ7.J2446Lo 1994 [E]—dc20 93-38765
A CIP catalogue record for this book is
available from The British Library.

The illustrations in this book were created
with pen-and-ink and watercolor.
Book design and hand lettering by Marilyn Janovitz
ISBN 1-55858-249-5 (trade binding)
1 3 5 7 9 TB 10 8 6 4 2
ISBN 1-55858-250-9 (library binding)
1 3 5 7 9 LB 10 8 6 4 2
ISBN 1-55858-702-0 (paperback)
1 3 5 7 9 PB 10 8 6 4 2
Printed in Belgium

For more information about our books, and the authors and artists
who create them, visit our web site: http://www.northsouth.com

To
Mario

Snail slipped

and hit bird.

Bird flew

and frightened frog.

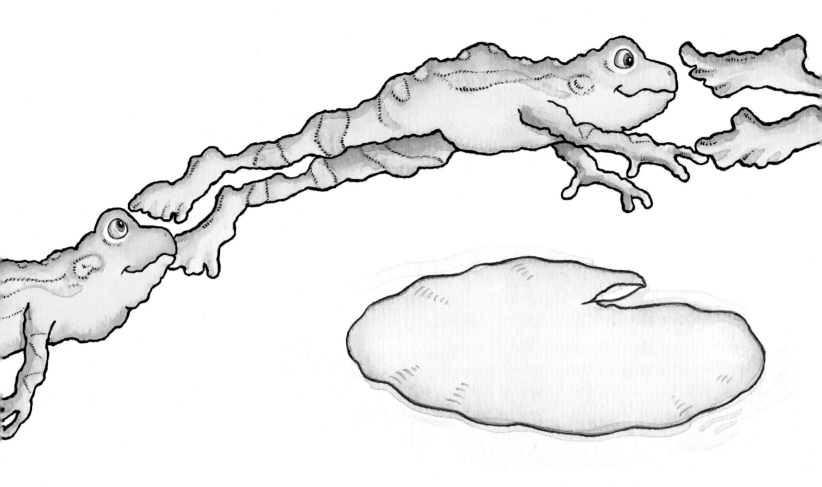

Frog jumped

and toppled turtle.

Turtle swam

and splashed salamander.

Salamander scurried

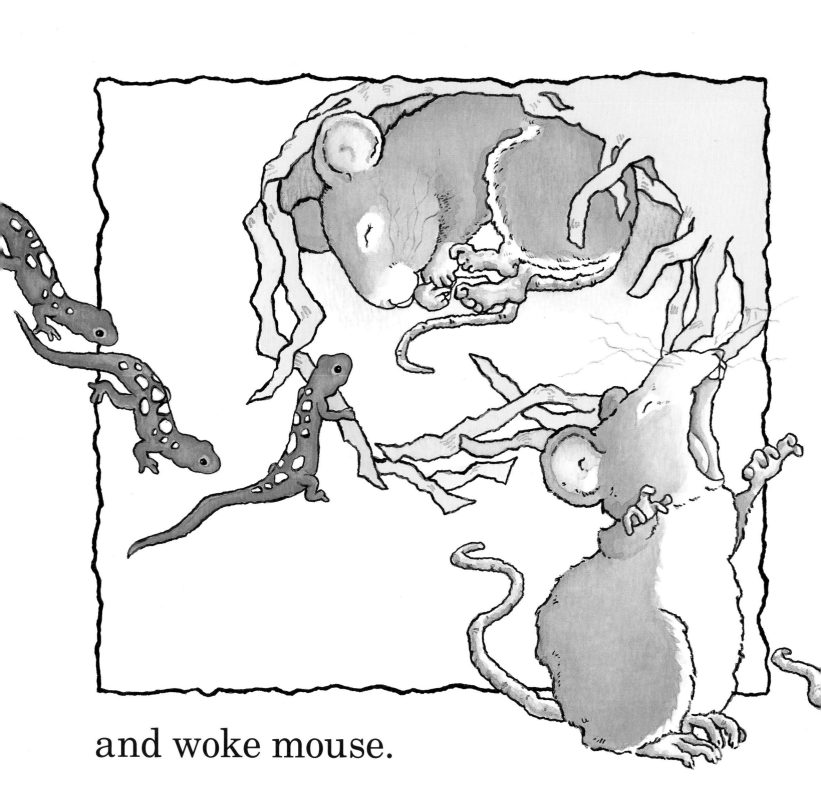

and woke mouse.

Mouse sniffed

and bothered bee.

Bee buzzed

and stung beaver.

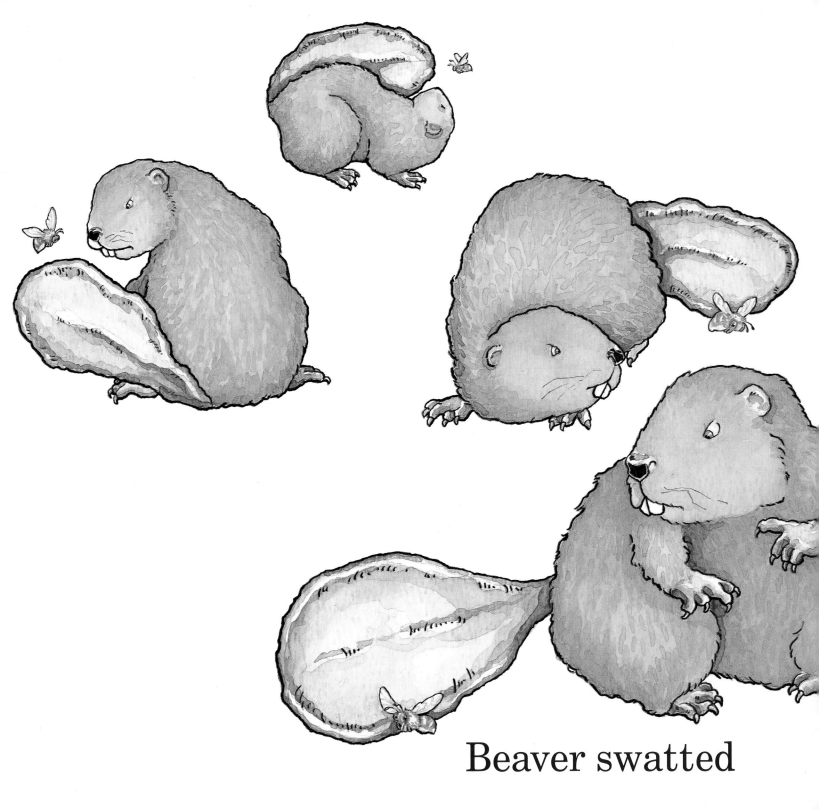

Beaver swatted

and slapped snake.

Snake slithered

and bumped beetle.

Beetle wobbled

and tickled toad.

Toad hopped

and knocked duck.

Duck dived

and flipped fish.

Fish flopped

and spattered moth.

Moth fluttered

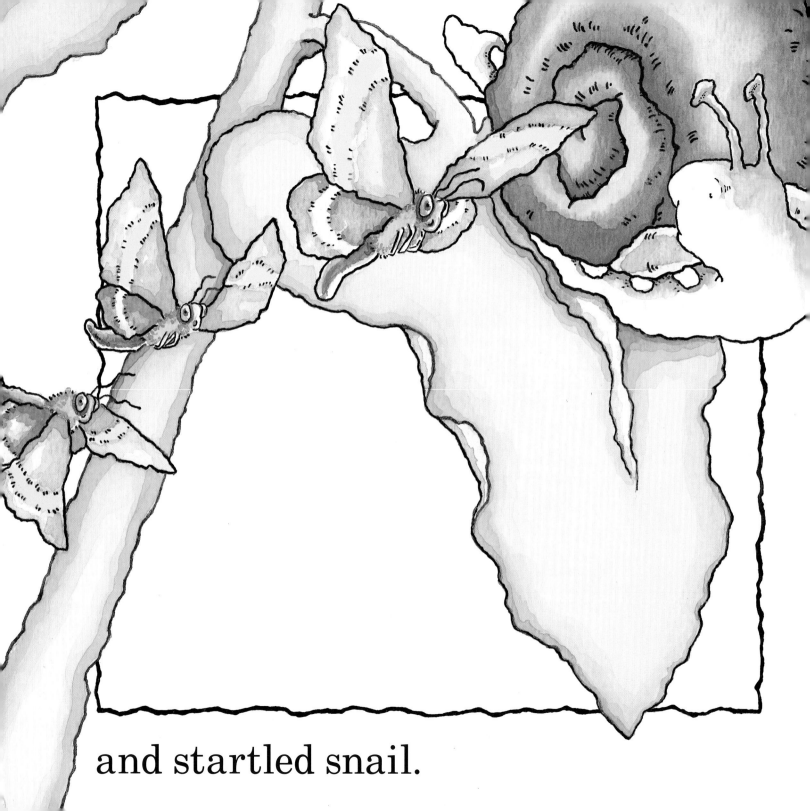

and startled snail.

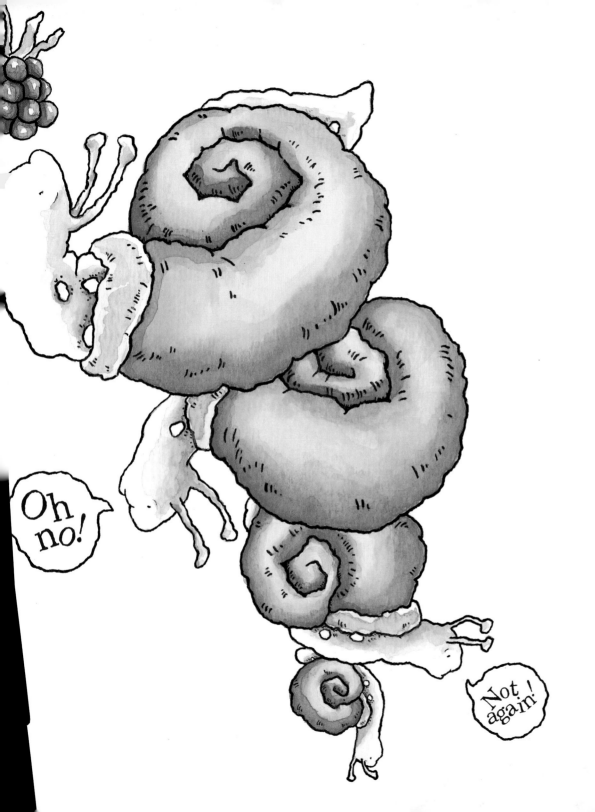